BOOK TWO

THE INFAMOUS RATSOS

Are Not Afraid

Kara LaReau

illustrated by Matt Myers

CANDLEWICK PRESS

Text copyright © 2017 by Kara LaReau
Illustrations copyright © 2017 by Matt Myers

First paperback edition 2018

Library of Congress Catalog Card Number 2017953740
ISBN 978-0-7636-7637-7 (hardcover)
ISBN 978-1-5362-0368-4 (paperback)

18 19 20 21 22 23 BVG 10 9 8 7 6 5 4 3 2 1

Printed in Berryville, VA, U.S.A.

This book was typeset in Scala.
The illustrations were done in ink and watercolor dye on paper.

Candlewick Press
99 Dover Street
Somerville, Massachusetts 02144

visit us at www.candlewick.com

For Catherine

K. L.

For Pat, who can find treasure
in any junk pile

M. M.

JUNK, JUNK, EVERYWHERE

This is Louie Ratso. This is Ralphie
Ratso.

The Ratso brothers are walking
home from the Big City Carnival.

"I love the carnival," Ralphie says.
He takes an extra-big bite of his cotton
candy.

"Me, too," says Louie. "I love the rides and the food and the games in the arcade."

"The arcade games are my favorite," Ralphie says. "I love the ringtoss and the whack-a-mole and the rope climb and the fortune-teller and the high striker. And the prizes."

"There's only one thing I don't love about the carnival," Louie says. "The

fact that it only happens once a year. I wish we could go there every day."

When the Ratsos reach their neighborhood, they walk extra fast as they pass the Haunted House. That's what all the kids in the neighborhood call the run-down house on the corner. They say a ghost lives there who only comes out at night.

Louie always gets goose bumps when he walks past the Haunted House. He doesn't tell Ralphie this. Louie is the older brother, so he is supposed to be the braver one.

"Whoa . . . that's a lot of junk," Ralphie says. He points to the lot next to the Haunted House. Louie has never really noticed the lot because he's too busy trying to hide his goose bumps. But if there is one thing the Ratsos love, it's junk, especially someone else's old junk. And this lot is full of it.

Before the Ratsos know it, they are rummaging through the junk piles. And before Louie Ratso knows it, his brain is working on something.

"I know that look," Ralphie says. "You have an idea."

"Yep. A big one," says Louie.

"Um . . . does it involve cleaning?" Ralphie asks. Cleaning is Ralphie's least-favorite activity.

"It does," says Louie. "But it's going to be fun. Trust me."

Ralphie considers the mess all around them. "Where do we start?"

"First, we'll need help," Louie says.

"A lot of it."

FUN TIME

When we're done cleaning, I think we should build a clubhouse," suggests Tiny Crawley.

"I think we should plant a garden," says Fluffy Rabbitski. "With lettuce and carrots and cucumbers."

"We should bring a bunch of tents and sleeping bags here and camp out. We can make s'mores!" says Chad Badgerton.

"All of those are good ideas," says Louie Ratso. "But I have a *great* idea. We're going to turn this into . . . the Big City FunTime Arcade!"

"What's an arcade?" Fluffy asks.

"It's where you play video games," Tiny explains. "Are we going to play video games here?"

"Not video games," Louie explains. "This arcade will have *carnival* games."

"Like the arcade at the Big City Carnival?" Ralphie asks.

"Yep. But the Big City Carnival only comes around once a year," Louie reminds them. "The Big City FunTime Arcade will be around all year long!"

"How are we going to turn *this* into an arcade?" Chad asks.

"I have it all planned out," Louie says. "We'll make the games using some of this junk, and we'll clear out the rest. We'll have an entrance, where we'll sell tickets."

"And we have to have prizes. Lots
of prizes," Ralphie says.

"I figure we can give away our old toys," Louie says. "When we make enough money from the tickets, we can buy better stuff."

"I have lots of old toys at home," says Tiny.

"Me, too," says Fluffy.

"Excellent. OK, back to work, team!" shouts Louie. "First we clean. Then we build. Then we *play*!"

"What about all the old furniture over there?" Chad says. He points to the pile of junk closest to the Haunted

House. Just looking in the direction of the house gives Louie a wave of goose bumps. He pretends to consult his plans extra carefully.

"You take care of it, Chad," Louie says.

"Why don't *you* take care of it?" Chad asks.

"I'm *supervising*," Louie says.

"I thought we were supposed to be a team," Chad says. "Or maybe you're *afraid* to go over there?"

"I'm not afraid," says Louie. "I just have a lot of work to oversee."

Chad's stomach growls. "We'd better
be done soon. It's almost dinnertime,"
he says. The Ratsos used to think Chad
was mean, until they realized he gets

cranky when he's hungry, which is almost all the time.

"Never fear," says Ralphie. "I brought emergency snacks for Chad."

As Chad eats and cleans, Louie glances up at the house. He swears he sees something white move behind one of the boarded-up windows. Louie shivers. Did he just see . . . a ghost?

– 3 –
RALPHIE LOVES STINKY

The next day is a Monday. The Ratsos hate Mondays. Ralphie hates this Monday in particular, because he has a spelling test.

In the middle of the test, Ralphie hears something roll under his chair.

It's a purple pen. The purple pen belongs to Stinky Stanko, the girl who sits behind him. Ralphie picks it up and hands it to her, but he makes sure not to touch her. Everyone knows Stinky Stanko stinks.

"Thank you," says Stinky.

"You're welcome," mumbles Ralphie. He goes back to trying to spell the word *trepidation.*

By lunchtime, Ralphie is pretty sure this is the worst Monday ever. Everyone in the lunchroom seems to be singing the same song. The song happens to be about him.

"Ralphie and Stinky up in a tree, K-I-S-S-I-N-G!"

"Is it true?" Tiny asks him. "Do you really have a thing for Stinky Stanko?"

Ralphie pinches his nose. "P.U.," he says.

"Who is Stinky Stanko?" asks Fluffy.

"Her," Louie says. He points out Stinky, sitting at a table by herself. "She's in Ralphie's class. Everyone knows she smells bad, so no one will go near her."

"Is her name really *Stinky*?" asks Fluffy.

"That's just her nickname— though I don't even know what her real name is," says Tiny.

"Ralphie loves Stinky! Ralphie loves Stinky!" chants Kurt Musky.

"I do not! She STINKS!" shouts Ralphie.

"If you don't like her, why does everyone think you do?" asks Tiny.

"I don't *know*," says Ralphie. "All I did was pick up her pen during the spelling test today. That's what I get for being nice."

"MWAH! MWAH! MWAH!" Sid Chitterer makes big, wet kissing noises.

Ralphie tries covering his ears. He tries shutting his eyes. Nothing seems to help. It seems as if everyone in the lunchroom is laughing and pointing at him.

"I hate Mondays," Ralphie says.

"Don't let it get to you," Louie says. "Remember, we have an arcade to build after school. Stay focused!"

"Easy for you to say," Ralphie says.

- 4 -

BONES

I don't like this game," Tiny says. "Maybe you should find someone else."

"You're perfect for it. Who else are we going to get to be the mouse for whack-a-mouse?"

"I could do it," Chad says.

"We'd need bigger holes," Ralphie

points out. "And a different name."

Louie makes notes on his clipboard. "I'll work on it. Tiny, we can move you to the rope climb."

"But I'm afraid of heights," Tiny says.

Louie sighs. "You can give out the tickets. Are you afraid of tickets?"

"Not usually," says Tiny.

"What about me?" asks Fluffy.

"I have something special in mind for you," Louie says. He brings Fluffy over to a refrigerator box with a big hole cut in it. "You're going to be a fortune-teller!"

"But . . . I don't know how to tell fortunes," Fluffy admits.

"It doesn't matter. You just make stuff up," Louie says. "We're going to call you . . . *Madame Rabbitski!*"

"Ooh, that sounds mysterious. I like it!" Fluffy says.

"We need more room for the ring-toss," Ralphie notes. "If we spread out

any more, we'll end up in the Haunted House's yard."

"Maybe one of us should ask the owner if we can use the yard," Fluffy suggests.

"Sounds like a job for our *supervisor,*" Chad says.

Everyone looks at Louie. Louie forces himself to look over at the Haunted House. It *would* give them more room if they could use its yard. But that would mean he'd have to go up and ring the doorbell.

Louie swallows hard. He takes a few steps toward the front door. But the closer he gets, the more he thinks he hears noises.

Rattle, rattle . . . clatter, clatter . . .

Maybe it's bones, Louie thinks. *The bones of other kids who made the mistake of ringing the doorbell.*

Louie makes a big show of looking up at the sky and checking his watch.

"Let's call it a day, team," he says. "It's getting dark—and we don't want Chad to be late for dinner."

WHO'S THE BOSS?

Louie and Ralphie's father, Big Lou, has made his specialty for dinner — spaghetti and meatballs.

"So . . . what's new at school, boys?" Big Lou asks. He makes sure to give

everyone's meatballs a generous sprinkle of Parmesan cheese.

"Ralphie has a girlfriend," says Louie.

Ralphie groans. "I do NOT," he says.

"There's nothing wrong with liking a girl," Big Lou says. "Your mama was a girl. When I first met her I was just about your age, Ralphie."

The Ratsos take a moment to think about Mama Ratso. Even though she's gone, she's always in their hearts.

"Well, I don't like *this* girl. At ALL," says Ralphie. "Her name is Stinky

Stanko, and she STINKS. For some

reason, everyone at school is saying

I like her. Which I DON'T. Except for handing her a pen today, I've never even gone near her."

"No one has," says Louie.

"Then how do you know she stinks?" Big Lou asks.

"There are some things you just *know*," Ralphie says.

"Like that the house next to our arcade is haunted," Louie blurts. Just saying the word *haunted* gives him the creeps.

"Haunted?" Big Lou grunts. "Some-one's living there. At least, they used

to, years ago. Wonder what happened to them?"

"Maybe the *ghost* got them," Ralphie suggests.

"HA!" Big Lou laughs. "There's no such thing as ghosts," he says. "I've never seen one. Have you?"

Ralphie shakes his head and laughs, too. "I'm not afraid of anything," he says.

"Really? I'm afraid of lots of things," Big Lou admits.

"You are?" says Louie.

"Sure," Big Lou says. "Spiders, for one. They give me the creeps."

Louie and Ralphie shudder. Spiders *are* creepy.

"I just tell myself it's OK to be afraid," says Big Lou. "And I try to be brave."

"How?" asks Louie.

"By reminding myself that *I'm* the boss of me, not my fears," Big Lou explains.

"I might be afraid of two things," Ralphie admits. "Stinky Stanko, and people thinking I like her."

"Maybe you both need to tell your fears who's boss," says Big Lou.

"Maybe I need to have another meatball," says Ralphie, holding out his plate. "With extra sprinkly cheese."

Louie tries to focus on his dinner, but with such a lump in his throat, he can't eat. How can he tell a *ghost* he's the boss?

THE WRITING ON THE WALL

Tiny Crawley corners Ralphie as soon as he arrives at school.

"Is it true?" he asks.

"Is what true?" asks Ralphie.

"That you walked Stinky Stanko home from school yesterday?" Tiny says. "And that you were *holding her hand?*"

Ralphie drops his schoolbag. He stands on the front steps of the school. "ATTENTION, EVERYONE!" he shouts.

"I DO NOT LIKE STINKY STANKO.
I REPEAT: *I DO NOT LIKE STINKY
STANKO!*"

"Then why were you walking
her home and holding her hand
yesterday?" Sid Chitterer says.

"I wasn't! I wasn't!" Ralphie insists.

It's no use. Everyone is already
laughing.

"This stinks. In more ways than
one," says Ralphie.

"The more you deny it, the worse
it's going to get," says Louie.

"But what else can I do?" Ralphie asks.

Louie stops to think. "Well, someone has to be starting these rumors. Maybe you need to find out who it is."

"I know exactly where to start," says Ralphie. He marches over to Kurt Musky.

"What's up, lover boy?" says Kurt.

"Who's the one who's been telling you about me and Stinky?" asks Ralphie.

"I heard it from Sid," says Kurt.

Sid Chitterer tells Ralphie he heard it from his brother, Mitt. Mitt heard it from Velma Diggs.

"I didn't hear it from anyone," Velma says. "I saw it written on the wall in the girls' room."

"I've hit a wall. Literally," Ralphie tells his friends at lunch. "How can I find out who started the rumor now?"

"Maybe we need to see what's written on the wall," says Louie.

"But it's in the *girls' room*," Tiny reminds them. "That's off-limits to us."

"Not to all of us," says Louie.

Everyone at the table gets quiet.
Fluffy looks up from her pickled-beet-
and-eggplant sandwich.

"What?" she says. "Why are you all
looking at me?"

"You're needed for an important
mission," Ralphie says.

After lunch, the Ratso brothers wait outside the girls' room while Fluffy goes inside. She comes out a few minutes later, shaking her head.

"It says 'Ralphie Ratso likes Stinky Stanko,' and then it says 'R.R. walked S.S. home from school yesterday and held her hand.'"

"Go back in there and get rid of it!" Ralphie shouts, pushing Fluffy toward the door.

"I tried already," says Fluffy. "It's written in purple ink that doesn't wash off."

"Written in *purple*?" says Ralphie. He smacks his forehead. "I'll be right back."

Ralphie goes back into the lunch-room. Everyone else has already gone back to class. Except for Stinky Stanko.

"Why did you start those rumors about me?" he asks her.

"How did you know?" she asks.

"The purple ink on the girls' room wall. It came from your purple pen, didn't it?" Ralphie says.

Stinky sighs. "Everyone likes you," she says. "I figured if people thought you liked me, then they'd like me, too. No one has wanted to be friends with me since people started calling me 'Stinky,' which made everyone assume that I stink. So I thought I'd start my own rumor."

Ralphie blinks.

"I'm really sorry," Stinky says. She starts to cry. "Are you going to tell everyone it was me?"

Ralphie isn't thinking about telling anyone. He's remembering who started the rumor about Stinky. It was *him,* back when he and Louie were trying to act tough all the time. He was joking around with Kurt and Sid when he made up the nickname "Stinky Stanko." At the time, it just

sounded really funny. But it doesn't
seem funny at all now.

"I think I'm the one who's sorry,"
Ralphie says.

DING!
CRASH!

Earth to Ralphie," Chad says. "Are you going to try to whack me, or what?"

Unlike Chad, Ralphie can't seem to keep his head in the game. He keeps thinking about Stinky, and about the look on her face when he told her he was the one who first came up with

her terrible nickname. She'd been crying, but when he told her, she'd stopped. She had looked him in the eye and said, "The one who really stinks is YOU, Ralphie Ratso!"

Ralphie has never felt more rotten in his life. What feels even worse is knowing he deserves to feel this way.

"Madame Rabbitski sees . . . a headache in Chad's future," Fluffy says. Even though her "crystal ball" is just a spray-painted fishbowl, she's getting pretty good at fortune-telling.

"This mallet is bigger than me. How will I ever ring the bell?" Tiny says.

"Just hit it as hard as you can," Louie says. "We need to make sure all these games work before the big opening."

"OK, here goes nothing," Tiny says.
He swings the mallet. When it comes
down, the bell rings.

DING!

And then it goes flying.

CRASH! goes a window in the Haunted House.

"Uh-oh," Tiny says.

"Madame Rabbitski sees . . . a tough break in Tiny's future," Fluffy says.

"In everyone's future," Chad says. "That bell was the only thing here that wasn't made of junk. We don't have any money to buy another one."

"That was our best game, too," says Ralphie.

"Not so fast," Louie says. He looks up at the house. The broken window looks like a glaring eye.

"Are you really going to go get it?" Ralphie asks.

Louie doesn't answer. He is already walking up to the house. *It's OK to be afraid,* he tells himself. He takes a deep breath and presses the doorbell.

At first, Louie doesn't hear anything. Maybe the doorbell doesn't work. Or maybe it makes a sound that only the ghosts can hear. As goose bumps prickle up and down Louie's arms, he remembers what Big Lou said.

I'm the boss, I'm the boss, Louie tells himself.

From inside the house, he can hear noises.

Rattle, rattle . . . clatter, clatter . . .

Don't run. Don't run, Louie tells himself. But he couldn't run if he tried; his feet feel like two blocks of cement.

Suddenly, the rattling and clattering stop. The front door opens.

Creeeeeeeeeeaaaaaak . . .

And then, Louie sees—

A pair of red eyes staring right at him!

NUTS, NUTS, AND MORE NUTS

It really is a ghost! Louie thinks.

He's about to scream, but then he realizes that the pair of red eyes is attached to a face. The face belongs to

a little old man. The old man is pale and white—paler and whiter than anyone Louie has ever seen.

"Can I help you?" the old man asks.

Louie stands up straight. He takes a deep breath. "My friends and I were playing a game next door, and our bell went through your window," he explains. "May I please get it back?"

The little old man squints at Louie.

"My eyes aren't so good, so you'll have to find it yourself," he says. "Come on in, sonny boy. My name is Mr. Nutzel, by the way."

"I'm Louie Ratso," Louie says as he follows Mr. Nutzel inside.

Louie can't believe his eyes. No wonder there was so much furniture and junk piled outside the house — the inside is filled with nothing but nuts. Acorns, peanuts, hazelnuts, pecans, and almonds rattle and clatter around Louie as he makes his way through the rooms. *Those must have been the sounds I've been hearing,* he thinks. *It's not ghosts or bones — it's NUTS!*

Louie follows Mr. Nutzel up the stairs. Everywhere he looks, he sees nuts, nuts, and more nuts. "Did you collect all these, sir?" Louie asks.

"I did," says Mr. Nutzel. "I still do. But only at night; the sunlight bothers my eyes."

Louie realizes that the ghost everyone thought they were seeing was probably Mr. Nutzel, gathering at night. All this time, everyone has been afraid of a little old man. Everyone, including Louie.

Up in the attic, on top of a large pile of dusty acorns, is the bell. Louie picks

it up and dusts it off. "Thanks, Mr. Nutzel. We're really sorry about your window. We can pay to get it fixed."

"Don't worry about it," the old man says. "Spending some time with you was payment enough. I don't get many visitors these days. It's almost as if people are afraid of me."

"Maybe you could come to the arcade we built," Louie suggests. "We're having our grand opening on Saturday, and everyone is invited."

Mr. Nutzel shakes his head. "I wish I could," he says. "It makes me happy to see that lot so clean, and to know that you kids are enjoying it. But I can't go out in the sun with my eyes the way they are. I can't do much of anything anymore."

Louie looks out the attic window and sees Ralphie and Fluffy and Chad and Tiny down at the arcade, waiting for him. He gives them a wave.

"Well, I should be going," he says. "We need to finish getting ready for the grand opening. It was nice meeting you, Mr. Nutzel."

"You, too, sonny boy," Mr. Nutzel says. "Come back any time."

"Are you OK?" Tiny asks when Louie returns. "We were about to decide which one of us was going to run for help."

"I'm fine. And I got our bell back," Louie says.

"Hooray!" says Fluffy.

"I can't believe you just walked up to the door like that," Ralphie says. "Weren't you afraid of the ghost?"

"I was afraid," Louie admits. "But I told my fear who's boss. It turns out the ghost is just an old man named Mr. Nutzel. He seemed pretty lonely and sad."

"Can he help us get rid of the rest of this junk?" Tiny asks. "We could fit more people if we had more room."

"I don't know if Mr. Nutzel can help us, but I know a way we can help him," Louie says.

Ralphie looks up at his brother. He knows a way he can help someone, too — and be brave like Louie.

RALPHIE TAKES A STAND

I have nothing to say to you, Ralphie Ratso," Stinky says when he approaches her in the lunchroom. She turns away from him and eats her sandwich.

Ralphie looks around the lunch-room and imagines all his friends

laughing at him. *I'm afraid,* he thinks. *But I'm also brave.*

"Well, *I* have something to say," Ralphie says. He climbs up on the seat next to Stinky and faces the rest of the lunchroom. He takes a deep breath.

"ATTENTION, EVERYONE!" he shouts. "I WANT YOU ALL TO KNOW THAT I'M NOT CALLING STINKY STANKO 'STINKY' ANYMORE. I'M GOING TO CALL HER BY HER REAL NAME. . . ." Ralphie leans down. "What *is* your real name?" he whispers to Stinky.

"Millicent," she says.

"HER NAME IS MILLICENT," Ralphie continues, "AND SHE IS A NICE PERSON AND SHE DOESN'T SMELL ANY WORSE THAN THE REST OF US. AND IF ANYONE IS MEAN TO HER FROM NOW ON, YOU'RE GOING TO HAVE TO ANSWER TO ME."

After that last part, Ralphie gives the stink eye to Kurt and Sid. They sink down in their seats.

"You didn't have to do that," Millicent says as Ralphie climbs down.

"Actually, I did," he says.

"How can I thank you?" she asks.

"You don't have to," Ralphie says.
"But if you want, you can come with
me tomorrow. Do you like games?"

BRAVE TOGETHER

I don't know about this," Millicent says.

"It'll be great," says Ralphie.

"But what if your friends don't like me? What if they don't want to be friends with me?" she asks.

"If they're really *my* friends, they'll want to be *your* friend," Ralphie says.

"I'm afraid," Millicent says.

Ralphie takes her hand. "Let's be brave together," he says.

"Is this Millicent?" Tiny asks. "Nice to meet you! I'm Tiny."

"Nice to meet you, too," says Millicent. She shakes his hand, and Louie's, and Fluffy's, and Chad's.

"Wow, you don't stink at all. Actually, you smell kind of nice," says Chad.

"Watch it," says Ralphie, giving him a nudge.

"It's OK," says Millicent. "I do smell nice. I make my own perfume. I call this one *Vanillicent*."

"Mmm," says Fluffy.

"Maybe you could make some perfume for prizes," Louie suggests. "Do you want to work the prize booth?"

"Sure!" says Millicent.

"Let's do this. All this vanilla perfume is making me hungry," says Chad.

"Uh-oh," says Ralphie, reaching for the emergency snacks.

"I'll be right back. I need to do one more thing," says Louie.

Louie runs up the steps of Mr. Nutzel's house and rings the doorbell. A few moments later, he hears rattling and clattering, and the door opens.

"Hello there, sonny boy," Mr. Nutzel says, squinting. "Did you lose your bell again?"

"No," says Louie. "I made you something."

He shows Mr. Nutzel a special chair that Louie has made just for him.

"This way, you can be outside without hurting your eyes. You can watch all the action at the arcade," Louie explains.

"That's very kind of you," says Mr. Nutzel. "But I don't know . . . I haven't been out in a while. . . ."

"It's OK to be afraid," Louie says. "Being brave is hard. Believe me, I know."

"Ready for the grand opening, kids?" Big Lou says.

"Dad!" shouts Ralphie. "You came!"

"I did, and I brought my truck, so I can take all this junk to the dump," Big Lou says. "And my tools, so I can fix Mr. Nutzel's window."

"What's in the cooler?" asks Louie.

"Lemonade, popcorn, and oatmeal walnut cookies," Big Lou says. "You can't have an arcade without a refreshment stand."

"Mmm," says Chad. *"Refreshments."*

"Did you say . . . oatmeal *walnut* cookies?" Mr. Nutzel asks Big Lou.

"Madame Rabbitski sees . . . a future filled with sweet rewards," Fluffy says.

"Ladies and gentlemen, boys
and girls!" Louie shouts.

"The Big City FunTime Arcade
is open for business!"

Kara LaReau is the author of the
Infamous Ratsos series, illustrated by
Matt Myers, as well as the middle-grade
series the Unintentional Adventures of the
Bland Sisters, illustrated by Jen Hill. She
is also the author of several picture books,
including *Otto: The Boy Who Loved Cars,*
illustrated by Scott Magoon. About this
book, she says, "I hope Louie and Ralphie's
latest adventure shows readers that there's
no shame in being afraid. What's *really*
scary is when we let our fears get the best
of us." Kara LaReau lives in Providence,
Rhode Island.

Matt Myers is the illustrator of the Infamous Ratsos series by Kara LaReau, *E-I-E-I-O: How Old MacDonald Got His Farm (with a Little Help from a Hen)* by Judy Sierra, and *Pirate's Perfect Pet* by Beth Ferry, as well as many other books for young readers. About this book, he says, "My big fear was swimming. At first I was scared of the water, but soon I became more afraid of other kids finding out I couldn't swim. Now I love swimming and wish I hadn't taken so long to find out!" Matt Myers lives in Charlotte, North Carolina.

From accidental good deeds to affairs of the heart, there's always something to do around the neighborhood with the Infamous Ratsos!

www.candlewick.com

Are Not Afraid